Dollars to Doughnuts

a Novel

Shakir Mack

GPBM Publications

8730 Cincinnati-Dayton Rd. #755 West Chester, OH 45069

Manufactured in the United States Of America

Cover design: AZ / Ges / Nitelite Studio

Editor: Ges / Ariel Yisrael

Library of Congress has cataloged: Shakir Mack:

Dollars To Doughnuts: a novel/ 1't. ed.

p. cm.

ISBN 978-0-578-24378-8 (PBk)

This novel is dedicated to my parents...

Chapter 1

"Listen Cody, I've given you the benefit of the doubt for well over a year. I'm sorry, but this isn't going to work for me any longer."

"But Anna, you told me that you..."

Anna chimed in, "what, loved you? That was last week's news. Cody I'm seeing someone else, so I suggest you do the same."

The call went dead. Sitting on a plastic crate behind Chicken King, Cody peered at his phone in disbelief. He could not believe the woman he had been head over heels for the past fourteen months had dumped him so blatantly over the phone. He wanted to slam his phone to the concrete, but he knew it would take months to get a new one. His heart sunk to its lowest point as he smelled the off-putting stench of trash lingering from the nearby dumpster. He wanted to go dive inside of it and sob for the next few days. Before the sudden somber became pervasive he heard the granting voice of his boss, "Cody!" he clamored.

I wish I could quit this stinking job, Cody said within.

Later that evening while cleaning the dining room Cody heard the pestering voice once again. He was annoyed as he entered the small office. "Yes Mr. King, what is it now?"

Sitting behind his desk stuffing his face with a chicken tender was the oversized, mid-fifties, deadpan owner of Chicken King. He peered up at Cody and with a half full mouth he mocked him, "what is it now? Son I believe that's the last thing you want to be asking me." Mr. King dipped another chicken tender into the barbecue sauce devouring half of it. "Did you work on register three all day?" he asked Cody.

"Yes, I always work register three."

"That's what I figured."

"What's all this about? My register is spot on. In nearly fifteen months of me working here it's never been short."

"Well sport, that may have a ton of truth to it. But you see these here?" Mr. King held up nine twenty-dollar bills. "You know what these are?" asked Mr. King firmly.

"Yeah, twenty dollar bills."

"Gosh darn it, you're really smart! Yet blind as a blue bat. These here buddy are counterfeit twenties. Nine of them to be exact. Which means you were either in on it, or you're just flat out stupid!"

"Now hold on Mr. King, I didn't have anything to do with..."

"I don't want to hear it!"

"But..."

"Nothing! Nada! Zip it! Now listen here Cody, this is one hundred and eighty dollars in fake money. Which means register number three is that many dollars short. So guess what — it's coming out of your check."

"No way! I didn't have anything to do with that!" Mr. King finished the remainder of the chicken finger. "Come on Mr. King, you know I'm an honest worker."

"May be true however, you're still responsible. It's coming out of your check."

"Mr. King my rent is due next week. I cannot afford to pay a hundred and eighty dollars. Specially for something I had no dealings in."

"So are you saying you're not paying?"

"Yes I am! Cause I'm not in the wrong here."

"Ok, you're fired."

"Now just hold on Mr. King. Let's not make this into something bigger than it has to be."

"Too late. It is settled. Here is your last paycheck. Now exit the premises."

"But Mr. King..."

"No butts. You are no longer an employee at the world's famous Chicken King. Now beat it!"

As Cody exited the office he kicked over the water machine and slammed the door shattering the glass.

Chapter 2

The next morning Cody awoke around eight a.m. being that his body was programmed to awake two hours before he had to be at work. He looked around the old, unfinished basement that he rented from 65 year-old Mrs. Kramer and fell sour. The previous day had turned out to be one of the worst of his 22 years on earth. Cody sat up and took a long stretch. "Oh boy, good morning to the pits. How did the walls collapse in one day? Sheeesh — life sucks!"

After a morning crap, a lukewarm shower and old chicken tenders for breakfast Cody made his way upstairs. As apart of the agreement to receive a discounted price of $350 dollars a month and no utilities, Cody agreed to clean the kitchen and take out the trash daily. In addition, he was responsible for mowing the yard twice a month. While loading the dishwasher Cody began to mumble, "world famous Chicken King! Yeah right, that fat prick wishes. He only has one location. How does that constitute as world famous? Jerk."

"Well I see someone's not excited about something this morning."

Cody flinched, "Oh hey Mrs. Kramer. Didn't hear you enter."

"I may be sixty-five, but I'm still light on my feet." Cody found a much-needed smile. He then retrieved the morning paper followed by pouring her a cup of coffee. "Sleep well last night?" she asked.

"I've had better nights."

Mrs. Kramer popped open the paper. "Women problems?"

How could she know? "Umm no, just small tinkers, no biggies."

"How's work?"

Ok, does she know my entire bummed out yesterday or what? I have to lie. If I tell her I got fired she may kick me out. "Work is work. It's paying the bills. How's the coffee?"

"Steaming, smells good though. You know Cody; I am more than just your landlord. I'm your friend. You can tell me anything without being judged."

"I know. And I promise if the wheels ever fall off my wagon, you'll be the first to know."

After cleaning and taking out the trash Cody hopped on his moped and made his way to the Day Labor Headquarters. The line was long causing him to contemplate riding past but he decided against it. It took nearly an hour before he made it to the desk where a woman with dirty blonde hair and long, colorful fingernails sat reading a magazine. "Umm, excuse me. I'm here for day labor," said Cody frustrated.

Without removing her eyes from the magazine the dirty blonde replied, "sorry, all the day jobs have been filled. Come back tomorrow at eight a.m. Next!"

Cody climbed back onto his moped beyond flustered. His day was starting from yesterday's conclusion. He turned the key only to hear the moped stutter. He then peered inside the gas tank. "This is just wonderful—out of gas. Who the heck stole my rabbits foot?"

After a ten-minute hike to the gas station he put two of his last five dollars into the tank. It was approaching noon and for the first time in nearly fifteen months he had no clue what to do on a Thursday. He never took days off, nor was he offered any by Mr. King. Not wanting to waste his gas he thought about going back home to hide in the basement for the next few weeks. Instead he landed at his best friend's place. "What's up Cody? Tell me you scored on a scratch off. You, not at work? Something isn't right."

Lightly Cody tapped on the small bottle sprinkling fish food into the fish tank. "I got fired yesterday."

"Good for you. Chicken King is a crappy place. And so is the owner."

"Yeah, but it was all I had."

"Dude, I don't get you. You bypassed the code on my Z-Phone 10, then jail-broke it. You are a freakin' genius! You could easily get a job at a major tech company."

"Nah, not my thing."

"Cody you're a real project. You would rather ask customers, would you like any sauce with your tenders, than to make thousands doing something that comes natural to you. Dude you're a brain. Own it."

Gently Cody tapped the glass of the fish tank. "Keith I think this one is dead."

"Dude, did you just hear what I said?" asked Keith.

"Yeah I heard you. And the last twelve times as well. I'll be ok." Cody then walked up to Keith's physical training dummy giving it multiple blows to the ribs and face until he was almost out of breath. "Anna broke up with me yesterday."

"Get out! What the heck happened?"

"Beats me. She just phoned on my lunch break and told me I was old news."

"Damn bro. That sucks! Two whammies in one day. Wanna go out and get wasted?"

"No thanks. But you know what would help? Isabella," said Cody.

"Uh, what about Isabella?" hesitantly Keith asked.

"Let me take her out tonight."

Keith stood silent then spoke, "Cody we're one-hundred percent bros! However, Isabella, you know my dad gave me that bike. I'm sorry, but I never let anyone ride her."

"I understand. I'm about to roll. Catch you later."

Chapter 3

As Cody sped top speed on his moped he uttered, "well Betsy, no Isabella today. That's cool, you're fast enough for me baby."

Fifteen minutes later he landed at Flower Manor retirement homes. "Hey Cody how's it been?" asked a female nurse.

"I'll lie and say lemonade while beach side."

"Well at least the vision is there right?" She said.

"You bet," Cody lied.

Moments later quietly he entered room 700. Once within the living quarters he spotted the spitting image of himself, 40 years his senior napping in a La-Z-Boy. He did his usual: checking the bathroom, kitchen, and closet area to assure all were cleansed and tidy. Ten minutes later Cody was removed from yesterday's reverie by a light cough. He turned to see his father slowly waking. "Hey Dad, enjoy your nap?"

Wiping the sleep from his eyes his dad replied, "Nathan is that you?"

"No dad, it's me Cody."

"Cody? Cody from Nam?"

"No, Cody from Florence."

"Florence, Italy?" Dad uttered.

Cody replied, "no Dad, your late wife Florence."

"Florence—aw yeah. Florence, my lovely butterfly. How's she doing son?"

"She's ok, just resting dad. Just resting."

"Cody is that you?"

"Yeah it's me. I came to see how you're doing and to handle a few of your affairs."

"Now there's a word you better not say in front of your mother. She swore up and down back in seventy-nine that I was having an affair with Mildred Miller from the sheriff's department. Can you fix me a cup of coffee son? Teaspoon of sugar..."

Cody chimed in, "tablespoon of cream."

"That-a-boy."

After downing half a cup of coffee with his father Cody broke the silence. "Anna broke up with me yesterday."

"Good, she wasn't my type of gal anyhow."

"Dad how can you say that when you never met her?"

"Exactly. Any gal seeing my Cody would have come visit the man responsible for your charming features." Cody fell into a chuckle. Dad then reached into his back pocket handing Cody a check that read, $3,200. "Hurry up and put that away son! Jennifer will be here any minute now."

Cody did as his father said and pocketed the veteran's check he received monthly. It was not until one day he asked his dad for fifty dollars and found out who, what, and why Jennifer was his Dad's so-called girlfriend. Twenty-six years younger, and stunning in her own way. It became obvious that she was only around for one thing—Dad's check. Cody stepped in and produced Power of Attorney forms causing Jennifer to call him everything but a child of God. Since then no one has seen or heard from her. Yet, Dad awaits daily for her arrival. "Well old man, I'm going to get going. Can I borrow sixty bucks?"

"Did you ask your mother?"

Cody sighed; he hated to see his father suffering from

Alzheimer's. Howbeit, he knew he had to give false responses to keep him calm. His mother had passed away 5 years ago.
"Yeah, but she told me to ask you."
Dad fell into a chuckle. "Typical Florence. Sure son. Take a hundred. What is mine is yours. And tell your mother to come see me at once."
   "Sure will Dad. Call if you need me. Otherwise I'll be back on Saturday."

   Cody gave his dad a firm handshake considering that dad did not believe in father, son cheek smooches. As Cody was leaving Dad uttered, "Cody, always hitch your wagon to a star."

Chapter 4

The next morning Cody arrived at the Day Labor Headquarters around 6:45 a.m. He told himself, *better to wait in line an hour early, than an hour late for nothing.* Soon he was appointed a day job at a local recycling plant. Little did he know it, but he was about to work like never before in hazardous conditions. Forced to wear a mask and eyewear to keep all of the grim and grit from clogging his nasal and eyelids he grew uneasy in no time. For hours he separated plastic, glass, aluminum, cardboard and paper. In the midst of doing such he saw baby pampers full of poop, used tampons, dead rodents and many other rotten yuckies. Seven hours later he was more than happy to call it a day. As he stood in line waiting for his check he thought about going back to Chicken King to ask for his job back. Before the thought had time to resonate he heard, "next."

"Cody Hyatt," he told the receptionist.

She handed him a check and spoke, "good work on the assembly line. Be here before eight a.m. on Monday if you want to work again."

Cody peered at the check and furrowed his brows. He was no rocket scientist, but one thing he did claim was mathematics. "Hey man keep it moving," came from behind.

Instead of making a fuss Cody slowly away mumbling, "seven hours for forty-seven, twenty-five. This is bullshit!" he brassed off while exiting the building.

As the warm sun beat against his face Cody left speeding in frustration. "Forty-seven measly bucks to search through crap for seven hours. Jerks! That's not even minimum wage. Day labor is a rip off, screw that place! Maybe Keith is right, I should go work for a tech company. Yeah right, dream on! Who's going to hire a tall, skinny kid with no degree? Who am I fooling? What am I going to do to make money?"

The next morning Cody entered the bank. The line held three customers before him. He peered to his right to see if the pleasure to his eyes was at her desk. His insides celebrated as he saw the business banker with blonde streaks talking to a client. *Gosh I wish I was in her league. She's a total babe!* "Excuse me, you're next," came from behind.

"Oh, I'm sorry," said Cody as he rushed to teller number four.

"Welcome to Second Community. How may I assist you this morning?" asked the female bank teller.

"I have a deposit. And I need to cash these two checks."

"Sure. So how have you been? I haven't seen you in a while," said the female bank teller.

Caught off guard Cody ran his hands through his hair and replied, "good I guess."

"To guess is one of life's more riskier hollow points."

"Well since you put it that way, I've been fine. Thanks for asking."

"How would you like your money?"

"Large bills will be fine. And can I withdraw one hundred dollars from this account?"

"It's a beautiful day out. You can have anything you like."

Cody found the teller's response to be flirtatious. Minutes after all the transactions were complete the teller asked, "anything else I can help you with Mr. Hyatt?"

"No thanks, enjoy your day ma'am."

Before exiting the bank Cody peered over to steal one last look at the business banker that he was crushing on and nearly tripped and fell over an unseen step.

Chapter 5

One of Cody's favorite pastimes was shopping at Sal-Mart in the wee hours. He loved searching the aisles and imagining all the things he could buy once he was able to afford a place of his own. At 1:30 a.m. the mega shopping store was nearly empty, besides workers restocking the shelves. Cody landed in the electronics department. He loved testing out whatever video game was on display. Moreover, Barbra with the freckles and square glasses worked nights. "Hey Cody. I looked for you last week. You were a no show."

"Hey Barb. Yeah I had to work a double and I was beat."

"Sounds like you're working towards a goal."

"Uh, not really. The only goal I have these days is to keep from becoming homeless."

"Oh stop it with your worthless, self-pity spill. My door is always open. I've told you that a gazillion times already. Hey guess what?"

"What's that."

"You sure you're ready for this?" asked Barbra followed by a goofy chuckle.

"Spit it out already," Cody ordered.

"I get my braces removed next week. We 'have' to celebrate. Wanna go out for pizza and wings?"

Even though he wasn't in the mood to hang out he decided not to hurt her feelings. "That's awesome Barb. Is Friday ok?"

"Yeah it's perfect, because I'm off Saturday. And after pizza and wings maybe we could go back to my place and hang out. That is, if it's ok with Anna."

Cody paused for a moment then continued playing the video game. "She dumped me," Cody muttered.

"What?" she asked.

"I got tele-dumped on my lunch break."

"That bitch! How dare she dump you over the phone? At least she could have come to your job and done it in person."

"Gee thanks Barb," Cody said glumly.

Barbra rushed to stand beside him gently rubbing his back. "Oh Cody, I'm sorry—I didn't mean to bite the injury. Want to hang out until I get off at five, then go to breakfast?"

"Thanks Barb, you're such a genuine friend. However, I had a long day. I'll call you soon."

"Sure, I understand." As Cody walked away Barbra stated, "you're my only true friend Cody. I'm here if you need me."

As Cody rode through the quiet night he smiled thinking about Barbra. She was the purest person he had ever met. She always made him smile and managed to remain happy despite being labeled as a pariah along side a life of being bullied and called the *Freckled Face Fink*. Now three months into the glorious age of twenty-one, Cody was not only her truest friend, he was her only friend.

Cody landed at the gas station to fuel his two-gallon moped tank. While doing so he stared at a group of guys pulling off in a luxury sedan. He fantasized for a moment and after then he heard, "PSST."

He snapped out of fantasyland and turned around. To his surprise it was a pleasant one. "Umm, hey—where do I know you from?" asked Cody.

"Let me see, should I feel insulted?" Cody stood disoriented. "You honestly don't remember?" Cody shook his head no. "I helped you the other day. I work at Second Community Bank." Cody slapped his forehead with his palm. "Duh, that's right. Sorry, but forgive me, you look... different."

"In a good or bad way?" she asked.

She is so hot! But way out of my league. What am I supposed to say? "Great, no answer. Which means a bad way."

"No, no, no! That's totally not what it means. You look, nice." The bank teller smiled. "Nice, that's new."

"No, nice in a good way, I mean great way."

"Ok, that makes me feel a little better. So what are you doing out at one-thirty in the morning?" she asked.

"Uh, just coming from Stal-Mart. I kind of like to shop at night."

"Me too," she exclaimed.

"No way. So are you coming from there?"

"Not tonight. I just left a party that was thrown for one of my colleagues."

"Sounds like fun."

"Corporate bore. I could have been entertained some other way, you know?" Cody nodded. "So what are you about to get into?" she asked.

Ha, who, me? Oh-my-god, like what am I supposed to say? Cody said within. "Uh, I was just about to head home and eat a pack of Twizzlers before dozing off."

Behind an honest smile the bank teller said, "I like you Mr. Hyatt, and also confess to loving Twizzlers myself. Hey, how about we head back to my place for a glass of wine?" Cody's knees suddenly felt wobbly. He took hold of his moped for support. His ears had to be playing tricks on him. Before he could answer she said, "I'll take that as a yes. Follow me."

Chapter 6

A million thoughts raced through Cody's mind as he followed behind what looked to be a fairly new Audi. For a moment he wondered if he was dreaming until he hit a cold patch as he traveled down hill on a dark road. A while later they turned into a subdivision with a sign that read: Fairfield Oaks from the 300's. *Holy Crap!* Cody said within. Two turns right and one left, brought Cody's eyes to the opening of a garage door. "Whoa!" he muttered.

Seconds later the bank teller exited the Audi A6 and waved Cody in. "Come on, I believe that'll fit," she uttered. Once inside the home Cody's eyes went wandering in sure amazement. This was by far the nicest home he had ever set foot in. "Hey, kick off your shoes, pull out the Twizzlers and make yourself comfortable."

"Umm, I'm sorry — but I think we have a slight problem," said Cody. The bank teller removed her shoes, sat her purse on the table and made way into the kitchen. "Slight problem, oh gosh don't tell me you don't have any condoms," she stated. Cody froze as his mouth fell agape followed by a foreign sensation that raced throughout his body. The bank teller turned to look at him. "Hey, I'm only Joshin'. What's the spoil?"
Cody exhaled and hurriedly gathered himself. "I don't have any Twizzlers. They're at my house. Sorry!"
The bank teller waved him off, opened a cabinet, and tossed

Cody a pack. "Now that we have that settled I have a confession of my own."

Cody somehow found quick humor and said, "don't tell me you're not wearing any panties." *Oh God, why did I just say that?*

"Wow you're good. How'd you know?" she asked.

"I didn't, I was just being humorous. Sorry."

"Hey if you say sorry one more time I'm going to bop you. Anyhow, the spoiler is... that I only have Merlot. And I'm not in the mood for red wine. So I'll be fixing us a pitcher of cherry martinis. Agreeable?"

"Sure," Cody replied a bit frightened.

Before long they were settled on the couch sipping and eating Twizzlers. "This is an awesome combination. Thank you Mr. Hyatt."

"You know you can call me Cody."

"Sure thing Cody—and you can call me Madison." Cody smiled quickly then looked away. "Don't tell me you're nervous," said Madison.

"Ha, nervous. Aw no—I'm ok."

"Let me see your hand," Madison demanded. Hesitantly Cody granted her request. She gently held his hand and then said, "Liar."

"Ok, ok. I'll admit, I am a bit nervous. This is not the norm for me."

"Which part is weird? Us holding hands, or that it's in the middle of the night? Or being here alone with me?"

"Umm, I'm going to say all of the above," Cody mellowed then took a large gulp of his drink.

Madison chuckled. "Hey, just relax and be yourself. I'm no one to be afraid of."

Yeah that's easy for you to say. "So do you live here alone?"

19

"I sure do."

"Wow, this is a nice house, and pretty big too."

"Yeah it was a birthday gift to myself. So who do you live with?" Cody sat silently. "Wow, three seconds and no response. Girlfriend alert."

"Not quite, she uh, like dumped me a few days ago."

"Ouch! I guess someone needed a drink." Cody peered at the glass and took another sip. "Careful, the liquor is disguised. It'll creep up on you."

That's exactly what I need it to do, to calm my nerves.

After conversing about Cody's break up for several minutes he asked, "so why are you single?"

"Well let's see. I dated this jerk for three years and finally grew tired of his bull crap. So then I went to cherry town and start dating this gorgeous Argentinian woman for nearly a year. Then she decided to move back to her country. After that I went on a few dates but nothing worth putting in a journal, so here I sit." *Ok Cody you're so out of your league. She drives an Audi, lives in this huge house. She's getting hotter by the minute. 'And' she's dated a chic. No way she's into me!* "What are you thinking about?" asked Madison as she tugged at his ear. "Honesty is the way to a woman's heart."

Cody sighed aloud then peered at her and spoke, "honestly, I'm sitting here saying to myself, I can't be her type. She's way too hot, and I'm just plain ole me. So I'm lost wondering why am I here?"

Madison went for another Twizzler, bit off half, and said, "refill time—hold that thought." Five minutes later she returned with the pitcher full of Martinis. "Grab our glasses and follow me."

They went down a flight of stairs, through the basement and out a door. "Whoa!" said Cody.

Madison's back yard was garnished to the nines. There was a deck with a bar, a grill, outdoor couches, a lit fire pit, a pool and a Jacuzzi. "Are you still holding that thought?" asked Madison.

"Uh, yeah."

"Good, come on, let's get in the Jacuzzi." Without hesitation Madison removed her blouse then slid out of her pants. Cody's eyes nearly popped from the sockets when he saw that she was truly pantieless. However, she left on her sports bra. *Shit, I'm getting a hard-on,* Cody said within. "Come on, take off your clothes and get in." Madison commanded. Cody had never been so nervous in his life. He felt like turning around and dashing out of there. "I'm going to count to ten — and if you don't have your ass in here I'm going to yell at the top of my lungs." *This is just great. She'll laugh when she see my boxers. What have I gotten myself into?* Luckily due to the nervous impediment Cody's bullet point subdued allowing him to strip down to his boxers. "Nice six-pack. And even sexier boxers," said Madison as Cody eased into the Jacuzzi.

"Thanks, this is... really nice," said Cody.

"Yeah, I love it out here. It's so peaceful." Cody inhaled making sure that he savored the moment. Even though he knew he was not dreaming, it surely felt like he was. Madison refilled their drinks then held up her glass. "May I propose a toast?"

"Sure," said Cody as he followed suit.

"To the beauty of life, and propositions."

"I'll drink to that, I guess," said Cody with a raised brow.

The moon was nearly full and the stars shined with brilliance. Cody and Madison sat in silence looking upwards until she stated, "forever and a day, my dad used to tell me, Madie, always hitch your wagon to a star."

"Hey, my dad told me the exact saying just yesterday."

"How ironic. Proof to an organic connection. So are you still holding that thought?" she asked.

"Sure am. I mean I still don't get it."

Madison strummed through the water and decided to speak on another topic. "Do you have any set goals for the next, say twelve months?"

"Not really—honestly I would like to get my own place soon."

"So who do you live with now?" *Oh boy, I should tell her with Keith. She'll laugh if I tell her I stay in the basement of a sixty-five year-old lady's home.* "I stay with a friend of the family," Cody murmured.

"Hey, that's perfectly ok. Listen, I'm not here to judge you. And just because you see this nice home doesn't mean place me on some sort of pedestal. You can be yourself around me. I know you're twenty-two and work at Chicken King."

Cody ran his hand over his forehead. "Ok, so what is it that drove you to invite a regular guy like me over to your house?"

Madison sipped her drink then offered a seductive smile. Cody felt his loins becoming effusive. Next he felt Madison's foot ease up his leg. *No way! This isn't happening!* "Hmm, let's see. Why invite a regular guy like you to my home? Then into my Jacuzzi." Madison went for another sip then slowly shook her head. "You'll never imagine in a hundred years. However, I'll say this... I like you and... I, find you to be perfect. So, I would like to make you a proposition."

Chapter 7

As Cody awoke on the couch he slowly sat up looking around in awe. "Hey, what happened last night? I can't believe I fell asleep over here." Cody got to his feet then called Madison's name. He waited for her to appear but she never did. He decided to check the garage and found that her car was missing. He rushed back inside and discovered a note on the kitchen counter:

Cody,

Rise and shine. Hope you slept well. I really enjoyed your company last night. Thanks for the idea of adding Twizzlers with cocktails. I got called in to work early this morning, didn't want to wake you. If you're hungry help yourself to anything you find. Maybe if you're not busy we can get together again next Friday. Lock up when you leave.

P.S. I think you're perfect!
Madison,

***

When Cody made it home it was a little after 10 a.m. Mrs. Kramer was sitting at the kitchen table reading. "Morning, you and Anna must have made up?" she said from behind the newspaper.

"I wish. I stayed with a friend last night."

"Oh! Well there's some warm biscuits in the oven and homemade plum jelly in the window seal if you're hungry."

"I'd have to be insane to turn down that combination."

After devouring three biscuits, cleaning the kitchen and mowing the lawn Cody met Keith at a local Coffee and Tea shop. They settled on the back patio over Raspberry Tea. "Dude last night the strangest thing happened to me," said Cody.

"Don't tell me you used Barbra as a rebound, and she gave you the screw of your life?"

"No gutter brain. Me and Barbra are best friends. Platonic my I add. We'd never cross that line. And too, she's not my type."

"Dude I believe if Barbra took off those geek goggles, fixed her hair and got dressed up, she'd be super hot," said Keith.

"Not a chance," Cody countered. "Listen, last night I was at the gas station and this total babe from the bank approached me. Then somehow we ended up back at her place."

"Liar."

"Dude I'm being serious. So check this out. She drives an Audi and lives in this huge home all alone."

"Did you score?"

"Just listen. So before long we land in this 'super dope' back yard, and out of nowhere she takes off her pants and hop in her Jacuzzi. And dude, she didn't have on any panties. I nearly fainted."

"Come on Cody, tell me you scored."

Cody could only shake his head at his wayward best friend. "Anyhow, so we drank and talked for hours. It was a cool time."

"Hold up pause. You had a drink? As in liquor?" Cody nodded yes. "He's human!" Keith cheered. "So let me weigh this out correctly. She got you tipsy, then was inches away without panties. You and Anna are no longer an item, and you say this woman is hot. Of course you scored. So how was it?"

"I don't know, because I didn't score."

"Seriously, I really have to get you checked out."

"It's doesn't make sense for her to know where I work, know that I ride a moped and a few other lame offerings. Yet still invite me back over next Friday. What else could it be? Keith I think she's really into me."

Chapter 8

Friday came before Cody knew it. While visiting his dad he suddenly wondered how he would get in touch with Madison. He decided to swing by the bank to see if they were still on for the night. "Hey Dad I'm getting ready to leave. I have to stop by the bank before they close."

"Damnit Nathan, I don't need my clothes taken to the cleaners! Hold your got-darn horses! Joseph A. Bank? Hey, I heard they're having a sale. May as well buy me a new blazer." Cody pulled the covers up to his father's neck then patted him on the chest. "I'll see you in a bit Dad."

"Cody is that you?"

"Love you Dad. Get some rest."

Just as Cody was set to start his moped his phone rang. He answered without checking the caller ID. "Hey Cody—it's Friday, what time are we meeting up for pizza and wings?" *Oh no! Barbra. I totally forgot we were supposed to go out and celebrate. Shit!* "Hey Barb, I uh... I totally forgot about our plans. Please forgive me. I can't make it tonight. Can we reschedule?"

"Aw Cody. I made reservations for us at Leprino's."

"Barbra I'm so, so, so sorry! I promise I'll make it up to you."

"Well, I guess I'll just stay home and nuke some popcorn. I'll chat with you later." Barbra ended the call.

Cody felt terrible. He knew how important this was to Barbra.

She had only been saying it for the past two years that the moment she had her braces removed she wanted to go out and celebrate. As Cody sat feeling compunctious his phone rang again. He hoped it was Barbra. If so he was going to tell her that he would be there. Madison would just have to understand. "Well hello handsome."
Cody looked at his phone. "Umm, who would you like to speak to?" he asked.

"This super handsome guy name Cody."

"Ok... this is he, who's this?"

"Madison." *Whoa! How did she get my number?* "I know, how'd I get your number. I'll explain tonight. Meet me at my place, nine p.m. sharp. Attire casual. Chow!"

Once the call ended Cody sat on his moped in a world of confusion. The allure that she possessed told him not to think too hard. "Even though this is so out of the norm, just relax and go with the flow."

Chapter 9

Cody arrived at Madison's place five minutes till nine. After the second ringing of the doorbell he received a text: 'come in, it's open.' After entering he heard Madison utter from upstairs, "you're five minutes early. Very impressive. Be right down."

Once Madison made it downstairs Cody's eyes nearly formed cartoon hearts. Madison held a win-over smile as she did a 360 twirl. Beyond nervous Cody somehow spoke, "wow, you look..."

Hurriedly, Madison spoke, "you better not say nice."

Cody chuckled. "I was going to say that jokingly. But I'll say gorgeous."

"You sure this shirt isn't too bright?"

"No way — it brings out your eyes."

Madison found a blush, "I didn't know you were a charmer. A handsome one at that. Shall we?"

Before long they arrived at Revel's by the River. They were seated by the window that overlooked the southern current of the river. "This view is killer," said Cody.

"Indeed it is. Have you ever been here?" asked Madison.

Cody paused while pinching at his nose. "Umm, no. I've always wanted to dine here. But it's..."

"Hey, it's totally ok. This makes tonight a bit more special.

As I mentioned before, you can be yourself around me. I know who you are—and it's perfectly ok. So shall we order a bottle of champagne?"

"I uh, guess so."

"No need to panic, dinner's on me," Madison assured.

After ordering their meals and settling on their second flutes of bubbly Cody spoke. "Madison can I speak my mind?" She nodded. "Ok, it seems to me that you can have any man you want. Yet, you've invited me on a date that you're paying for. Clearly you're not desperate—and I'm no outrageously gorgeous guy. So please tell me what's going on?"

Madison took a sip then looked around the restaurant's dining room. "First of all, who are you to tell another's eyes what gorgeous looks like?"

They sat in silence for a moment. Suddenly the waitress appeared. Madison requested the check then took Cody by the hand but not before sneaking the half full bottle of champagne out with them. They landed on a bench near the bank of the river. "I can't believe you snuck out that bottle."

"What's a girl to do, leave our mouths dry?" she replied.

"Gosh you're..." Cody caught himself before saying what he honestly wanted to say.

"I'm what. Nice?"

They chuckled. "Aw what the hell. You're fuckin' hot!"

Madison bit her bottom lip then took a hefty swig from the bottle. She then took Cody by the face and placed her lips against his. Before Cody's body had a chance to go numb Madison slowly transferred the champagne from her mouth to his. Cody's eyes went wide as his body yelped within. His brain could not register what had just transpired. He could not move or speak. "Are you ok?" asked Madison.

"Umm, I think so," Cody lied.

"Good, now you can return the favor." Madison handed him the bottle. Nervously he took a gulp then slowly made way to her lips. "Damn, that was sensual," said Madison as she swallowed the champagne. Cody suddenly stood to his feet and ran both hands through his hair. He exhaled while peering out into the racing current of the river. The night breeze was perfect. Nature was at her finest as the stars sparkled and the creeping creatures sounded of in rhythm. "Cody I love nature. I love its creator, and I really love this moment. It feels so natural. You're such a beautiful, regular guy, which makes you heaven sent. Do you know how long I've thought about this night?"

"How long? And why?" Cody asked.

"For nearly a year."

"Yeah right."

"It's true. I remember what you had on the day after your twenty-first birthday." Cody furrowed his brows, then turned towards her. "Hey listen, don't go freaking out on me and no I'm not a stalker. It was just something about you that I fell in love with the moment I laid eyes on you."

"Fell in love with?"

"Yes, you heard correctly. And yes I could have any guy I want. But I'm here and so are you — so what's that say?"

"What did I have on?" asked Cody.

"A grey T-shirt, Levi's and a pair of black and white Vans. *Whoa! That's what I wore the night before when Keith and I partied.* "Does your silence mean I'm correct?" asked Madison.

"How did you remember that?"

Madison smiled then took a swig. She then handed the bottle to Cody. "Listen Mr. Hyatt, when a woman has something or someone on her mind — she won't forget the slightest of details."

"Charmer," said Cody.

"Scaredy cat," Madison countered.

"Am not!"

"Come kiss me then."

"No."

Madison smiled then stood to her feet. "Don't worry, you'll change your mind." Madison found a rock and tossed it into the river. "Cody can I be blunt?"

"Haven't you been since we met?"

Madison shoved him gently. "Smart ass! Ok, so I'm thirty-eight and my clock is ticking away. And as the calendar ages, I've come to the conclusion that I'm tired of living alone." *Holy crap! What is she saying? Does she want me to move in? No way — we barely met just days ago.* "Remember the other day when I mentioned I had a proposition for you? If it's ok I'd like to share it."

"Sure, I'm all ears."

"How much do you make working at Chicken King?"

Cody found the question to be out of left field. And too, quite embarrassing to answer. "Really, do I have to answer that?"

"Hey, it's ok — I kind of like know already. Remember I cash your check sometimes."

"I uh, I make minimum wage."

"So that's like what, a little over fifteen thousand a year?"

"This is a bit embarrassing," Cody said.

"Cody I'm so not trying to belittle you. I'm, I'm... Oh gosh, how can I say this? Cody I want to offer you... a little over double what you make in a year."

"Ha!"

"Thirty-five grand."

"Thirty-five grand for what?" he asked.

Madison took a sip then handed the bottle to Cody. "Finish it." Cody did such then tossed the bottle into the river. "Can I hold your hand?" she asked. Cody slowly offered it. "Cody promise me before I say this that you are not going to flip out."

"Even though this is like a tab bit weird. I promise not to."

"Great. Cody I, I would like for you to... Oh boy! Cody I would like for you to help me, become a mother."

Chapter 10

The next morning Cody sped down the alley until landing at Keith's home. He killed the engine once in the backyard. Now at Keith's bedroom window which was never locked he gently raised it up. The bedroom was empty. Quickly Cody hoped inside quietly landing on his feet. Keith's couch bed was out with ruffled sheets. Cody sniffed trying to identify the lingering scent. Then out of nowhere a naked woman owning a lovely pair of C-cups came into the room. "Oh shit! Who are you?" she asked rather calmly. Cody stood mannequin, yet his eyes took a glance at her neatly shaved landing strip up to her perfect breast. His lower parts began to flinch. "Keith!" she bellowed. "You didn't tell me you were expecting company this morning."

"Hey listen I'm like totally sorry. I had no clue Keith had company," Cody said earnestly, then turned his head.

"Dude it's ok. I go nude on the beach every chance I get. These tits are happier free." *Don't forget gorgeous and pretty big*, Cody wanted to say. Suddenly he heard a loud pop. Keith had slapped the nude woman on the bottom. "Ouch!" she cried out.

"Kitchen please. You promised to cook breakfast," said Keith.

"Naked or apron?" she asked.

"Apron," Keith requested. She then left the room. "Cody you perv. You totally just saw my two-week-old girlfriend's rack."

"Dude where did you meet her at?" asked Cody.

"On the side of the highway. Her car had broke down, so I

gave her a ride home. Well to my home."

Cody stood agape then spoke, "she's bomb."

Keith stood clad in a pair of boxer shorts holding his tooth brush. "So what's up? What brings you through my window this morning?"

Being startled by the beautiful nude woman shifted Cody's thoughts. After shaking off the curl of one's hair, he remembered why he had come to his friend's place. The night before didn't seem real. Nevertheless, he knew what he heard and after confirmation, Madison repeated her request. Cody brushed past Keith, closed the bedroom door and began to whisper. "Dude, last night I had the most bizarre thing happen to me..."

Keith chimed in. "What. You got laid?"

"Shut up! No. I went on a date with that super hot lady from the bank."

"Ok, I know you got laid. How old is she?" Was it great? How's her rack?"

"Keith is your friend eating?" the woman uttered from the kitchen.

"Yes."

"No—I'm not hungry," Cody whispered.

"You are not hungry? Gosh-darnit! You didn't score."

"Dude, seriously. I'm in a quandary, and I need your help."

"Ok, ok simmer down. I know that look. So what happened?"

".... so after dinner, champagne and making out by the river she hit me with..." Cody fell silent then ran his hand over his face.

"Hit you with what?"

"A curve ball at two hundred miles per hour. Dude she asked me to knock her up."

"Hold up... As in pregnant? Beach-ball-belly?"

Cody sighed then said, "I need a glass of cold O.J."

Cody found himself sitting at the kitchen table with a shirtless Keith, and the beautiful woman who only wore an apron. As she forked her eggs over easy, both of her succulent breast hung freely. Cody could barely concentrate on eating from seeing such a sight. "Babe, Cody here is a rock star. Last night this super hot banker...." Cody tried to reach over and silence Keith but it was to no avail. "...she asked Cody to knock her up."

"Dude, really," Cody complained.

"Wow, Cody you must be something," she stated flirtatiously.

"Is he. He's more of a stud than me—because she offered him thirty-five grand."

The woman's eyes went wide. "Did you just say thirty-five gees?" Keith nodded yes. "Wow, you must be..." the woman caught herself before saying something out of place.

"Damnit Keith! I can't believe you just did that," Cody spout gruffly then stood up.

"Chill Cody. Heather's cool. It's no big deal." Cody shook his head then marched out the door. "Cody come back I'm sorry!"

Chapter 11

Thirty minutes later Cody found himself pressing the doorbell close to several times until the door finally opened. Cody formed a slight grin, nevertheless, he wasn't greeted with one in return. "Hey, unlock this screen door," said Cody.

"Why should I?"

"Because I'm your best friend."

"Yeah right. Best friends don't leave each other hanging."

"Hey—I know you're not mad about last night," Cody said.

"Sure I am. Now scram!"

"Make me! Cody countered.

"I will, don't test my alter ego."

"Come on Barb. Pretty please," he begged.

After a moment Barbra decided to allow him entrance. Cody rushed her from behind lifting her off her feet causing her to giggle. "Stop it Cody. You're going to drop me."

"Say you're sorry."

"No way, I didn't do anything."

"Ok, suit yourself." Cody gently dropped Barbra on the couch. Swiftly, she grabbed a pillow and struck him.

"That's for standing me up!" She popped him one last time. Cody was now laying on the floor. "Ok you win, I'm sorry. Will you ever be able to forgive me?"

"Humm, let's see. Only if you'll spend the entire day with me."

"No way!" Cody said. Barbra cocked the pillow ready to pop him again. Cody held out his hands, "hey I'm Joshin'! I would love to."

Barbra was all smiles as she held Cody around the waist as they sped at 35 mph through town. If there was a seventh heaven on earth, this was it for her. She loved riding shotgun with her best friend on his moped. It set her mind and concerns at ease. After eating brunch they landed at Tarjae. Holding hands while in tow Barbra questioned, "what are we doing here?"

Cody chose not to answer, yet turned and winked at her. Soon they were in the aisle that held all the teeth products. Cody asked lowly, "can I see your smile?" Barbra blushed turning maroon. She then checked her surroundings, they were alone. In a bashful manner she displayed her newly, straight-lined smile. "Holy crap!" Cody exclaimed.

Quickly Barbra covered her mouth. "What is it?" she muffled from behind her hand.

Cody stepped a bit closer and muttered, "your teeth... they're so perfect."

Barbra fell enamored and rushed Cody for a hug. "Really!" she asked.

"Really, times ten. Now allow me to buy you some new tooth brushes, whitener and floss picks."

Barbra displayed her luminous smile then hugged Cody tighter.

Later that evening as they ate pizza and wings Cody suddenly fell into a reverie as Barbra spoke about the latest *Milan Monthly*. His mind had been at peace hanging with Barbra until now. He started wondering what it would feel like to have thirty-five thousand dollars. He then questioned if he could really offer himself as a sperm donor for money. His mind then shifted to Madison's naked rear as she eased into the Jacuzzi. Her sleek cheek bones and slightly full lips. Her gorgeous green eyes, off-set by her dirty brown strands. Her home, her car, her maturity and her soft kiss. Suddenly his body tingled remembering the moment shared as Madison slowly transferred the champagne from her mouth to his. He felt his groin beginning to grow. "Cody! Earth to Cody," said Barbra.

"Sorry—what did you say?"

"I said, remember last year when you told me not to purchase those two Bitcoins?"

"Uh, yeah, I remember," said Cody.

"Cody what's on your mind? You've all of a sudden went slow-brain."

Cody couldn't dare tell her the truth so he quickly used his father as the reason. "I was just thinking about Dad."

"Oh gosh—I like so need to go see him. Will you take me soon?"

Cody smiled knowing that Barbra and his father got a kick out of each other. "Sure, we'll go in the next day or so."

"Great. So listen, last year I paid six-hundred bucks for two Bitcoins. And 'someone' said; why are you wasting your money? Well guess what—as of last week the Bitcoin is... hold up, excuse me Ms., can you bring us two Lemon Drops?"

Cody's mouth went agape. He'd only seen Barbra drink once since her twenty-first birthday, in which she swore never to do it again. "Barb what are you doing?"

"What's it look like? Celebrating with my best friend. My braces are gone forever and the Bitcoin in now eleven hundred per."

"Bull crap!" said Cody. Barbra grabbed her phone and quickly showed Cody the screen. "No freaking way!"

"Yes freakin' way! Now can I get my props as a great investor?"
Cody held an incredulous look then held out his fist for Barbra to touch.

Chapter 12

The next morning Cody awoke on the floor next to Barbra. After two drinks they were both three sheets to the wind and had to call an Uber. The buzzing sound of his phone caused him to roll over. After a morning stretch he grabbed his phone and saw that he had two missed calls and text messages:

I called you twice last night with hopes of inviting you over. Before I fell asleep I couldn't stop thinking about you. And don't you dare read this and say; why does she like me? Because I do, and because God only made one of you. That makes you 'Rare' - 'Priceless' - 'Endangered' and identified as 'TAILOR MADE.' Cody I'm sorry if I came off too fast, blunt, or even disrespectful. But I've mused on this for months and this is what I want. I hope I didn't scare you off. If for some reason you don't hate me, meet me at my house tonight at ten. –Madison.

Cody was now at home and found it to be strange that Mrs. Kraimer was not there. Normally when she left she would leave a sticky note on the refrigerator. Suddenly a knock came at the front door. Cody thought about letting it go unanswered but decided against it. When he opened the door a smile grew upon his face. It was eight-year-old Chris from four houses down. "Hey Cody what's up?"

"Not too much little guy."

"Whoa! From now on—let's lose the little guy. It's cute in some cases. But in mine, it hurts my reputation. I've grew an undisclosed amount in inches in just a few short weeks."

Cody fell into a chuckle. "Really! Can I ask you to forgive me?"

"Forgiven. Now here's the deal. I'm selling Christmas candy for my school. Twenty bucks and you're in. You'll save ten whole dollars."

"Chris it's September."

"Exactly. Reason being, if you wait to buy it in December the price will be through the roof."

"Gosh you're good. How can I say no?" said Cody.

Cody was set to reach into his pocket then he hesitated remembering that he was unemployed and just yesterday he spent $75 dollars entertaining Barbra. As much as he did not want to think about Madison's offer he could not help but to. *Oh-boy, thirty-five thousand. For sex, for my sperm. This is so odd. Far away from normal. But thirty-five big ones. Jeez, my life would become that much easier. What am I going to do?*

"So what's it going to be Cody? Time is money. I have more people to see."

"You're lucky I like you," said Cody as he produced a twenty-dollar bill. Once Chris pocketed the money he said, "thanks Cody, I'll see you soon." He hopped off the porch and ran away.

"Hey, what about the order form?" Cody whooped.

After a long, mind boggling day Cody decided to show up at Madison's home. It was five minutes till ten when he rung the bell. Seconds later he winced hearing, "it's open, come in." Madison directed him to her office. "Hey handsome. I'm so glad you came." She raced for a hug then gave him a peck on the lips. "Have a seat," she offered.

"Wow, this is a very nice office," said Cody as his eyes took stock of the room. "Yoooo! You went to the U of Conway?"

"Sure did. Cougars for life."

"I received an acceptance letter from them."

"No way! Why didn't you accept?"

Cody sat silently then spoke. "I, I had to take care of my dad."

Madison's heart melted. "See that's one of the reasons I adore you. You put your life on hold for your dad. Most people wouldn't do that."

"I'm all he has. The choice was easy."

Madison poured them two glasses of aged Bourbon and held her glass up for a toast. "To the blessings you'll receive in the near future."

As they conversed the alcohol had Cody mellowed out. "I did a lot of thinking today and honestly I'm on a seesaw. Apart of me wants to do it. But then I'm like no way."

"It's totally ok. Honestly I wouldn't feel comfortable if you didn't have mixed feelings. This is a major decision." Cody slowly sipped his drink then continued, "ok, say I go along with this. What would my role be as this child's father? Would we ever have a chance of becoming a couple? Or even..."

Madison took hold of her glass and downed the drink. followed by a refill. "Cody, I uh... I would like to raise my child alone."

"So that means the money is for my sperm? And in so many words—then get lost."

"Don't say it like that. I would let you see him or her, but not like all the time."

Cody's phone buzzed. After checking it he saw that he had a text:

I hate to bother you — but could you swing by. It's somewhat of an emergency.

"I'm sorry Madison, I have to go take care of something."

"Great, you hate me," she stated.

"No I don't. Honestly I have to run."

"Well I'll say this before you go. Next Thursday I'll be ovulating. So will you let me know your decision before Wednesday?"

Cody stood to his feet then nodded. "I'll think about it."

Chapter 13

The bourbon and Madison's indecent proposal had Cody's mind racing. He was extra cautious as he rode his moped to his destination. Once there his phone buzzed. The text message read:

I wish you would have stayed. We could have relaxed in the Jacuzzi, then cuddled on the couch. Come back if you want. :)

"Jeez, Madison is so hot. That just made me hornier than ever. Maybe I will head back over. Aw what the hell, I do need to get laid."

Slowly the front door opened. "Who are you out here talking to?" Barbra asked while holding a tall glass in her hand.

"No one. I was just thinking out loud," Cody lied.

"Ok Ed Sheeran," she teased. Soon they were in the kitchen as Barbra bragged about the Long Island ice tea recipe. She handed Cody one and began promoting it. "Listen, I assure you that it'll beat out the bartender's. If not I'll buy you the new Call of Duty next week."

"Deal," said Cody. After a few sips Cody could not lie. The drink was very tasty as well as strong. "Ok, props to you Barbra the Bartender."

Barbra chuckled, "told you. Can you believe this is my second one. I'm already feeling a bit..." Barbra paused then sipped.

"A bit what?" asked Cody.

"Vulnerable. I was about to call... Percy."

"What! Hell no!" Cody muked.

"Calm your knee caps. That's why I called you over. I think I'm drunk and I need you to keep me level headed." Cody began to laugh. "Don't laugh at me."

"I'm not, it's just I'm a bit boozed as well. I may just let you call him."

Barbra gently punched Cody in the arm. "If you do, I'll let you call Anna."

"Argh! I'd rather puke first," he declared.

"Liar. You still love her.

"Not true. Hey listen, today I was talking with an old friend and he told me the most bizarre thing ever."

"What, that his penis was missing?" said Barbra as she laughed at her own joke.

"No gutter brain. He said that this woman wants him to knock her up..."

Barbra chimed in, "I wish someone would knock me up! Hell I haven't had sex in over two years."

"T.M.I. Seriously, she wants him to get her pregnant, and in return she's going to pay him thirty-five grand. But here's the kicker. After donating his sperm she wants him to get lost."

"Oh—that's a new one," she said followed by a hefty gulp.

"So, do you think he should do it?"

"Cody I'm drunk. I don't know."

"Aw come on Barb. My friend is in a pickle."

"Why not. Tell him to go for it. Once the baby's born she'll change her mind about him getting lost. Now come on, I want to show you something." Barbra took Cody by the hand leading them to her bedroom. She flopped onto the bed and grabbed the remote control. Cody settled at the foot of the bed. "Ok, before I turn on the TV let's see who can down their drink the fastest," said Barbra.

"Call of Duty on the line," Cody said.

"Deal. But if you lose, you owe me three days of platonic amusement."

"Deal," Cody confirmed.

"On three," Barbra stated then spat, "three."

Cody lost then uttered, "you cheated. I want a rematch."

Cody won the next round and by now they were both bashed. Cody was laying at the foot of the bed. Barbra powered on the TV and sent Cody into shock. She had tuned on a porno. Cody's eyes became locked as he watched a gorgeous blonde take it doggy from a well-built guy. "Gosh he's hot," said Barbra. Cody didn't pay her statement any mind. The state of being inebriated and the intensity of the scene had him frozen. Suddenly he thought of Madison. His hormones were saying; *call a Uber right now!* He could not hold it and quickly shot stiff. Seconds later he decided to turn around and ask Barbra what made her turn on the porno. Cody had to blink twice at what he saw. "Barb is that..."

"Yes, it's a dildo!"

"Ok, this is a bit much. I'm about to uh, go and uh..."

"Can it! You're soused, and so am I. Stop being such a priest. It's only a porn."

"Only a porn. Well this porn has my cock rock hard. Oh gosh, I didn't just say that."

Barbra chuckled. "Your cock is hard and I'm soaked. So guess what? I'm about to use this dildo. Wanna watch?"

"Ha, what did you just say?"

"I said come lay next to me, pull out your cock and let's masturbate together." The liquor decided for Cody and within seconds he lay next to Barbra holding himself. He watched as

Barbra insert the dildo into her starvation. "Whoa! This feels great!" she exclaimed. She then peered at Cody. He decided to remove her glasses. This was only his second time seeing her without them. Oddly he found her to be attractive. *I have to be wasted because Barbra is hot!* "Cody I never knew you had such length."

"And I never knew you were this adventurous."

"Adventurous... Cody this dildo is resplendent. But I, I wanna feel the real thing," Barbra removed the dildo and tossed it on the floor.

"You what?" asked Cody.

Without answering Barbra rolled over until she was on top of Cody. "You heard me. Now move your hand."

Cody did as told. Barbra then took hold of him and slowly eased down. They hissed in unison and began to explore one another in passionate ways.

Chapter 14

Cody finally opened his eyes and felt as if someone had wacked him in the head with a bottle. The headache he felt was thundering. He vowed to never drink again. When he turned over he could not believe his eyes. At first he thought the night before was a dream until he saw Barbra partially undressed as the covers barely covered her. The light snore she produced told Cody she was still out of it. He stared at her flat stomach, then slowly made way up to her perfect sitting breast. Lastly, he landed on her innocent facial features. Oddly she still presented a glistering look even in his sober state. Then out of nowhere reality struck. *No way! We... no way! Me and Barbra had sex last night? But how? Shit, this was not supposed to happen. Screw this, I'm getting out of here.*

Thirty minutes later Cody made it home only to find a empty house again. After rushing to the medicine cabinet and swallowing a few pain pills his head finally began to calm. With caution he eased next to Mrs. Kramer's bedroom door. Finally he cracked the door open. Mrs. Kramer's bed was empty and neatly made as if it had not been slept in for days. The ringing of the phone caused Cody to flinch. After speaking with the caller his heart sunk. Notwithstanding, taking the pain medication was over rode and his head raced back into a spin. Cody pressed his back against the wall and slowly slid to the floor.

When Cody made it to the hospital Mrs. Kramer had already passed away. A massive stroke was the cause of death the doctor had explained. After gathering himself Cody rode his moped happy as a duck in Arizona. Gloom struck with no destination he finally grew tired and landed at Flowers Manor to see his father. Mrs. Kramer's sudden passing made him want to spend as much time with his father as possible. "Hey Dad, how are you today?"

"Nathan is that you?"

"No Dad it's me Cody."

"Cody? Which Cody? You better not be one of those gosh darn salesmen!" Cody sat silent. He thought about all the mornings he and Mrs. Kramer would sit at the kitchen table and talk about everything under the sun. His eyes welled up, but before a tear could escape his dad spoke in unison with the ringing of his cell phone. "Cody is that you son?"

"Yeah Dad it's me. Hello."

"Cody where are you? I puked my face out this morning. I've called you five times—are you ok?"

"Uh, no."

Barbra went into a whisper. "Cody did we..."

"Cody is that your mother on the phone?" Dad uttered.

"No Dad."

"Is it Jennifer? If so tell her to bring me some fried cod, malt vinegar and my VCR."

"Barbra can I call you back?"

"Cody you don't sound well. Are you mad at me?" Suddenly the call dropped.

"Damnit Cody! I need to speak with Florence before Jennifer makes it here."

"Dad, Jennifer is out-of-town for a while. She said she hopes you're not mad. And if you are she will understand.

49

Dad went into a sinister chuckle. "Mad, mad! Now that's a good one. Listen Cody, do you remember how to morse code like I taught you many years ago?"

"Sure Dad."

"Ok, I want you to send General Moorer a message and tell him that I have eyes on the Vietnamese and I'm requesting more ground troops. And as for Jennifer — tell her we're finished. I'm shipping out at o-eight-hundred hours."

Minutes later a knock came at the door. Cody rushed to open it. He froze as he was surprised by the visitor. "Hey... wasn't expecting you."

"Sorry. I heard your dad's voice and figured you were here. Can I come in?"

Cody showed Barbra in and suddenly felt awkward. "Mr. Hyatt!" Barbra spout as she rushed to give him a hug.

"Cody who's this woman? Your mother will have my nuts between a cracker if she finds her here."

Barbra turned to Cody offering a modest smile. She then revealed a Zero candy bar before Dad. "Barbra? Hey Cody look who is here. Oh boy this is a treat!" Dad said happily.

After laughing and conversing Dad finally fell back into a blank space. Cody had eased into the kitchen while Barbra and Dad enjoyed seeing one another. Soon Barbra made way into the kitchen. In a low mutter she spoke, "hey bud, how are you?"

Gripping a tea cup with both hands Cody replied lowly, "not so good."

"Is it because of what I think, happened last night?" Cody shook his head no. "Come on Cody, you can be honest with me. I'm so the blame. I should have never made those stupid long islands."

"They were good," Cody mumbled.

"What you say?"

"They were good. Moreover, no one is blaming you for anything. I had a wonderful time last night. However, Mrs. Kramer suffered a stroke and passed away."

"Oh no!" Barbra said then rushed to pull Cody into a hug. She held her best friend close to her heart.

Chapter 15

Days later Cody lay in the basement throwing a racquet ball against the wall. Now that Mrs. Kramer had passed he had no clue what his next move would be. How would he pay all the bills? Would he have to move? He was unemployed, and down to his last $530. He picked up the phone to call Mr. King to ask for his job back but hung up the phone. He thought of the day labor route. The memories of hard labor, low pay and filthy conditions quickly nixed that idea. "Life sucks!" Cody uttered then slung the ball into a hanging shirt. Just then he received a text:

Hey handsome, hope all is well. I called you a few times over the past couple days. Are you screening my calls? Haven't seen you come into the bank lately. Is everything ok at work? Well I won't keep you. Howsoever, today is Wednesday, and I was wondering if you made a decision yet? If you feel up to it, call me later. – Madison.

Cody sighed then rolled over and buried his face into his pillow.

***

At 11:15 p.m. Cody's fingers were rapidly at work as they operated the joystick in attempt to advance to the next level in Call of Duty. "Have a nice night," said Barbra as she handed a customer their receipt. She then made way over to Cody.

"He got me," Cody cried out.

"Relax. You're a professional gamer—you'll beat it the next time you play."

"Yeah if I only had the money to buy it."

"Why would you do that when you can just come to my place and play it."

Cody whipped his head around. "What did you just say?" Barbra held an honest smile. "No, don't tell me..."

She chimed in. "Even though the other night we broke even on the bet. I decided to get it for you anyway."

"Barb! You didn't have to do that."

"It's ok. Remember, I get discounts. Plus I know you really wanted it."

"Gosh I hate you," said Cody.

"Feeling is mutual," she countered. "Anyhow, I'm off tomorrow night. Wanna swing by and play it?"

Cody's mind suddenly dove into the gutter. "Umm, I don't know. You might put on another one of those flicks."

Hurriedly, Barbra looked around then muttered, "hey keep it down! And no I won't. The long islands made me do that."

"Is that so? Did the long island also make you buy that dildo?" Barbra peered around once again while turning maroon. "Dude stop it. Can we not talk about that here?"

Cody found a much-needed chuckle. "Ms. Adventurous. Ok I'll see you tomorrow."

Moments after leaving Stal-Mart Cody landed at the very gas station where he and Madison bumped into one another many nights ago. His thoughts began to race, then out of the blue he heard a motorcycle pull up. "Hey bro—nice moped," said Keith.

Cody shot him a bird. "Just because you're on Isabella, don't try to play me," Cody stated.

"Never in a million years would I do that! Sooner or later we're going to upgrade you." Cody thought about the thirty-five grand and knew that he could use it to purchase a new Harley tomorrow. "Hey Cody, I'm glad I bumped into you. Remember that hottie you saw naked at my place?" Cody nodded. "Well she's having a killer party at the lake. Come on let's head over."

Before long they were amongst close to forty party-goers, more women than men. A bonfire was going along with beer and music. Cody tried his best to stand his ground but Keith wouldn't take no for an answer. Cody slowly sipped on the beer feeling a bit relaxed until his thoughts began to raise questions: *what if I just do it? Who's to say it would happen how she's planning it? What if she falls in love with me? What am I going to do about my living conditions?* Keith came from the behind and wrapped his arm around Cody's neck. "Dude, so whatever happened with that hot banker? Please tell me that you're thirty-five grand richer."

"I wish."

"Gosh you're such a Sponge Bob. But don't trip. Tomorrow I'm going to personally take you to this chic's place and..."
Without reservation a woman snatched Keith by the arm pulling him into the lake. Cody smiled at his friend but could not stop thinking about Madison's proposition. Cody took another sip of the beer then muttered, "screw this, I have to go. It's time to make a decision."

Chapter 16

After riding for nearly twenty minutes Cody landed outside Madison's home. *Why am I here? I can't do this. Ok, just text her and let her know you're not accepting the offer.* Suddenly the garage door started to open. *Oh no!* Cody cried out within. He thought to start the moped and pull off but it was too late. The garage had opened completely and Madison came walking out. Halfway down the driveway she spoke, "Cody? What are you doing here? It's nearly one a.m."

Lost for words he stuttered, "I, I was just uh, just about to text you."

"Oh really?" She said as she sat the trash can by the curb.

"I uh, I honestly was."

"Well since you're here, wanna come inside and tell me what you were going to text me?"

Sitting at the kitchen island across from one another Cody spoke. "You look nice," Madison chuckled. Cody slapped his palm against his forehead.

"Hey it's ok, it's actually stated at the right time. No makeup, hairs a mess and I'm in my robe. So I'll happily take the compliment. So tell me what you were going to text me." Cody exhaled then spoke. "Well, I guess I know what that sigh means," said Madison.

"I'm... I'm still indecisive. One minute I don't want to, the next I do."

"Let me ask you this. Is the only thing making you consider the money?"

"No," he replied.

Madison's facial expression changed. "Wow, that's a surprise. So what else is it if I'm allowed to ask?"

"Can I keep that to myself?" he asked not wanting to tell her that Barbra said once the baby was born she'd change her mind.

"Sure you can. Come on, I want to show you something." Madison took Cody by the hand and led him to her office. Once inside she turned on the light and Cody's eyes widened. Madison made her way to the side of the desk. "Please, have a seat," she offered. Before him was the same bottle of champagne they shared at Revel's by the River, and a Contract Agreement. However, the most alluring, was the four bricks of money. "As you can see Cody, I'm kind of prepared—just in case."

Cody was trying his best to keep from looking at the money. He had never seen as much at one time. It was beyond tantalizing. How much is that?" he asked.

Madison looked at him for a moment then spoke, "Let's just say, there's a tip in there." Again they sat in silence. Cody ran his hand over his face. Madison gently sat an ink pen on the contract before Cody. His heart rate began to race. He felt beads of sweat beginning to form on his forehead. His hands began to shake, yet his thoughts became dauntless. They dared him to sign. Then pruriently Madison decided to dare him as well as enthrall. She stood and slowly let her robe to fall to the floor. Cody went numb, then swallowed the lump in his throat. Within he told himself to get the hell out of there, but was stuck to the chair. Madison began to ease from behind the desk causing Cody to swallow another lump. She moved to sit on his lap. Her breasts were now inches from his face. He had never saw a pair as succulent. He felt himself trying to burst through his pants.

Slowly Madison leaned forward and kissed him. She started nibbling on his ear then whispered. "Sign it, then take me upstairs and make love to me all night, and all morning, and all night again. Cody, I want you so bad!"

Cody's body went lava. The moment was nearly too much for him. He couldn't believe this gorgeous, perfectly built, sweet smelling lady was half naked on his lap ready to give herself to him. His mind was racing. Madison sensed it and grabbed the champagne, popped the cork and took a large gulp. She then refreshed his memory by transferring the champagne from her mouth to his. She repeated it a few times before taking a hefty gulp of her own. By now Cody could no longer take it. Without reservation he reached around her and signed the contract. This left Madison's expression in awe. Beyond excited she took another large gulp then transferred it into Cody's mouth. She sat the bottle down, took Cody by face and passionately kissed him. "Thank you Cody. It's a favorable contract. You'll thank me tomorrow. Now for the good part!"

Minutes later they were in her bed having carefree, hot, sweaty sex in each and every position ever thought of.

They went at it on an off all night, and morning. It was around noon when Cody finally kissed Madison goodbye. She thanked him for the twentieth time before seeing him off.

Once Cody made it home he raced to the basement and sat on the edge of his bed in silence for nearly five minutes. The love he and Madison made was beyond his wildest dreams. She had done things and positions that he never knew was possible. So much that he almost forgot about the money. At once he stood to his feet, took hold of the string bag and exhaled. Next he dumped the money on the bed. Before his eyes lay four bricks of cold cash, each were held together with $10,000 dollar wraps. The sight was so surreal Cody had to walk away from the moment. He could not believe he had agreed to be a sperm donor for money. He wondered if his mother was alive if she would approve of his decision. If Dad was in his right mind what would be his viewpoint of the situation. He sighed knowing that neither would approve. "Damnit!" he barked. "What did I do?" he asked himself while pacing the basement. "Ok, just simmer down. It's a possibility that it my not happen. Yeah, that's possible. Just relax—look at it on the bright side. All my worries are no longer. I'm really thirty-five grand richer." Cody rushed to the bed. He picked up the stacks of money and counted them. He did so twice. "No way! This is forty grand!" Cody fell confused until he remembered Madison's words. *Let's just say there's a tip in there. You'll thank me tomorrow!* "No way! Forty grand! She gave me an extra five thousand dollars?" Just then Cody's phone took off ringing. "Hello."

"You stood me up again."

"Oh no! Barb I'm so sorry!"

"Yeah, yeah, yeah. My feelings aren't important. I understand. I'm a geeky, freckled face, ugly nobody who work nights at Stal-Mat. Trust me I truly understand."

"Barbra! Don't say that. I hate when you talk about yourself that way."

"So what. It's true. Hey listen—I have to go."

"But Barbra..." The call went dead.

Cody tried to call back but was sent straight to voicemail.

Chapter 17

Nearly a week had passed since Cody had received the money from Madison. He also had not spoken with Barbra since he stood her up for the second time. It was close to midnight as he sat a red light minutes from Stal-Mart. His phone buzzed. "Hello handsome. Where are you?"

"About to pull up at Stal-Mart."

"How ironic. I just pulled into the parking lot. I'll wait on you."

After parking his moped Madison approached. "Great minds think alike," she stated owing an honest smile. Cody's loins became a bit excited from seeing her. He hadn't been in her presence since the magical night they shared. Madison noticed his body language to be some what nervous. "Are you ok handsome?"

"Who me? Oh yeah. Sure, yeah I'm fine."

"Liar," said Madison as she took him by the hand leading them into the store. As they surfed the aisles she spoke, "you know the other night was like beyond what I expected. I kind of want to do it again."

"Ha! What did you just say?" Cody asked in awe.

"You heard me. I want more. Is tonight too soon?" Before Cody could answer the bulge in his sweat pants spoke for him. Madison caught a glimpse before he quickly adjusted himself. "Oh boy—I guess that's a yes," she stated with a smile.

Before long they were approaching the electronics department. "Hey can we go get some Twizzlers?" Cody asked in a flap.

"Sure. Twizzlers, cocktails, and great sex. The perfect combination."

Madison turned the shopping cart around and they began to head to the food section, then from behind they heard a voice utter, "Cody?" Barbra stood silently.

"Who's she?" asked Madison.

"Ha! Oh, this is, my friend," Cody stated hesitantly. Barbra gave Madison a look over and instantly felt intimidated. Madison loomed class and money. In her silence Barbra turned and walked away. "Excuse me for a moment," Cody told Madison as he trotted after Barbra. Once he caught up to her he muttered, "hey, what's wrong?"

"What's it matter to you?" Barbra shouted.

"Excuse me, but did I do something wrong?" he asked.

"Now I see why you been standing me up," Barbra declared.

"It's not what you think. She and I are just friends."

"Just friends ha? That's bull crap Cody. She's too hot to just be your friend. I get it, I honestly do."

"Come one Barb, can I at least come by your place tomorrow so we can talk about it?"

"Cody shall I leave and let you and your friend talk?" said Madison as she now stood a few feet away.

"No, I mean—can I just have a moment?"

"No, go ahead. I have work to do," said Barbra as she made off between the double door.

Cody chased after her. "Barbra I came up her to bring you this." In hand Cody held a small box.

Barbra turned to face him. "I don't want to be friends anymore. Keep your stupid gift. Matter-of-fact, give it to her." With that being said Barbra walked off.

Later that night after drinks and Twizzlers, Cody and Madison shared in another blissful night.

Chapter 18

Eight Months Later...

      Cody had just served a customer at the Coffee & Tea shop where he now worked. He and Keith were such frequent patrons that when he asked the owner for a job he was hired on the spot. Even though he still had thirty grand of the money Madison had given him, he worked as if he was down to his last penny. Over the past several months a lot had changed for Cody. He was now taking classes at a local technical college, joined a fitness gym, found interest in penny stocks, and now rode a Sportster 883.

      After long days of school and work he normally went home and tampered with different electronic devices in the quiet basement of the late Mrs. Kramer where he still lived. With no surviving heirs the home was turned over to him. Some mornings he would still awake, wash the dishes and sit at the kitchen table reading the newspaper. He really missed Mrs. Kramer. She offered genuine love and wisdom when he needed it the most, and for that he would be forever grateful. As he sat sipping coffee and reading he came across Stal-Mart's sale section. Slowly he sat the paper down and began thinking of his best friend. It had been months since they last spoke. It pained him the night he showed up at her job and was told she no longer worked there. Then to make matters worse she changed her number and moved out of her place. Deep within he missed the hell out of Barbra. Little did she know aside from Keith, she was all he had in a friend. Cody's heart took a deep dive as he felt they were at a point of no return. On the other end of the pendulum he and Madison had fell mute. After their third sexual encounter Madison expressed to him that she no longer wanted to see him. At first he was hurt until he really thought about the grounds of their relationship. Though he had advanced financially and experienced the best sex of his life, deep within he bemoaned it, due to the fact it cost him his best friend.

After cutting the grass and checking on Dad, Cody was riding his motorcycle when his phone buzzed. It continued to buzz repeatedly causing him to pull over. "Hello, Cody speaking."

"Hello Mr. Hyatt. My name is Dr. Nicholas-Mead and I'm calling from Conway General. We have a Madison Ellison here and she has informed us as you being the father of her unborn child." Cody's ears went numb first slowly followed by his entire body. This was beyond news, being that Madison had never called or texted telling him that she had become pregnant. Momentarily his head began to spin. His mind fell blank as he suddenly began to shake. "Ms. Ellison has requested for you to come here as soon as possible."

Cody finally gathered himself and somehow built up the courage to head over to the hospital. Once he made it to the 4th floor he approached the nurses station. "Excuse me, "I'm looking for Madison Ellison. Dr. Nicholas-Mead told me to hurry here," Cody said nearly out of breath. The nurse ushered Cody to the delivery room. Seconds later a male doctor came out removing plastic gloves and his face guard. The nurse spoke, "Dr. Mead this is Mr. Hyatt."

Dr. Mead and Cody shook hands. "Mr. Hyatt would you like to put on a gown and head in?"

Cody was nervous however he nodded yes. Once he entered the room he froze. The first sight he saw was Madison laying in bed holding a small object that was covered up. A warm smile appeared on her face. Nevertheless, Cody remained in a frozen state. "It's ok sir, you can go stand next to her," said the nurse.

Once next to Madison she spoke in a groggily tone, "wanna hold her?"

Cody stood agape as Madison offered what was in the flesh, a beautiful, newborn, baby girl. Not fully understanding what was going on Cody's arms cautiously took hold of the small, fragile infant. "She's three weeks ahead of schedule so we'll need to get her upstairs in the next few moments," said the nurse.

Cody's eyes watched the little angel. His stupor was broken when Madison said, "thank you Cody. She's so beautiful."

Cody flinched at the sudden sound of machines in the room sounding. Madison's body started to jerk as the two nurses rushed to her side. "She's going into shock! Quick call Dr. Mead," said the nurse who brought Cody into the room. Then the other nurse spout, "her heart rate is racing and palpitating. We nee to stabilize her quick!"

Cody took a few steps back becoming extremely nervous. "What's happening?" he uttered.

"We're losing her!" Dr. Mead and another doctor appeared. They took the nurses spot and swiftly inserted a needle into Madison's arm. One of the nurses lead Cody and the newborn out of the room. "I need to get her upstairs," she stated gently removing her from Cody's arms. Cody stood in a daze.

Chapter 19

An hour later Cody was on his second cup of coffee as he paced the 4th floor hallways. He couldn't come to grips with what he had just witnessed. First he was hit with the surprising birth of his daughter that he never knew was in Madison's belly. His nerves were shot. Suddenly Dr. Mead appeared. Cody raced next to him. "How is she?" he asked on tenterhooks.

"I'm sorry Mr. Hyatt... she didn't make it."

"What do you mean she didn't make it?" Cody questioned.

"We did all we could, but her heart failed and we could not bring he back. I'm so sorry Mr. Hyatt." Dr. Mead turned and walked away.

Cody's face fell sour and his knees started to buckle. With caution he eased over to the wall and slid down to the floor. Everything had happed so sudden he didn't know whether to cry or scream, so he simply placed his head down and closed his eyes.

***

Four weeks later Cody was at work getting ready to close up for the evening. He way beyond excited knowing that his daughter who he had named Madison was set to come home tomorrow. "Alright Cody I'm gone, see you later," said his co-worker.

As Cody was set to lock the door and finish wiping the tables down the door came open. He bent down to pick up a straw from the floor. Without looking up he said, "sorry, we're closed for the evening."

"I was hoping for a cup of tea," a female stated. Cody froze. He longed to hear the voice. When he turned and looked up he could not believe his eyes. "Cody?"

"Oh-my-God! Barbra?"

Without hesitation she ran into his arms. The hug was long and fervent. Finally Cody pulled back so he could look at her. She had changed dramatically. Her hair was cut A La Mode. Her eyebrows were perfectly arched and her glasses were sleek giving her a look of professional sexy. Cody couldn't believe the transformation. "Wow! Barbra, you look wonderful!"

"So do you. Have you been lifting weights?" she asked bearing a smile.

Cody blushed. "A little. How have you been?"

"Mind if we talk over two cups of tea?" Barbra asked with a half-hearted grin. Moments later they sat smiling at one another. "Cody that night I saw you in Sal-Mat with that lady it made me feel unappreciated. I felt ugly being that she was so much prettier than me. It brought back so many bad memories. Cody it totally crushed the little self-esteem you helped me build."

Cody took her by the hand, "listen, never in a million years would I try belittle you. It was just a very confusing time in my life. Barbra you so mean the world to me."

Barbra fell into an honest blush. "You don't mean that."

"The hell I don't," Cody replied then rushed to the counter returning with a treat. "This is one of our signature Doughnuts. This is how much I care."

Barbra took the doughnut and bit into it. She then offered Cody a bite. "Ok, being that this doughnut is very tasty, I guess I believe you," she said warmly.

Cody checked his watch, "oh shucks—we have to get out of here. The alarm will automatically turn on in four minutes." With that being said Cody took Barbra by the hand and led her to his Sportster 883.

"No way! What happened to the moped?"

"I traded it in. Wanna go for a ride?"

As they cruised the dark back roads Barbra held Cody by the waist with her head pressed against his shoulder. She had forgot that this was her favorite place to be. After a fifteen-minute ride they landed at his place. Once in the basement Barbra spoke. "So this is the infamous man cave you've been residing in?"

"Yup, I love it down here. It's my escape from the real world." Barbra walked over to Cody's workstation where he had ton's of electronics sprawled out. "I see you're back doing what you love."

"Yeah, Keith talked me into it. So finish telling me what you've been up to."

"Do you have anything to drink?"

"Barely, I haven't really had a drink since..." He and Barbra looked at each other and both looked away with a slight smile.

After fixing them a drink they both sat on the bed, both Indian style. "Well, after that night at Stal-Mart I broke down and called Percy."

"No way!"

"Yes, I quit my job and moved in with him. He treated me fair for all of one month, then he became abusive. He started calling me ugly and did his best to make me feel like it. He broke my glasses calling me a geeked-out whore. He even brought another woman home. So I woke up one morning and left. I stayed in a women's shelter for two months. When I was there I met this elderly woman who spoke to my soul and taught me to love my flaws. And now here I sit — a brand new, self-confident woman." Listening to his best friend tell him about her highs and lows Cody couldn't help but lean forward to gently kiss her. Barbra soughed in pure pleasure and for the first time in months she felt safe. "Wow, that was nice," she mellowed. She then took a sip of her drink then fanned herself with her hand.

Cody smiled and said, "oh stop it. You're exaggerating."

"I'm not. Now it's your turn. I want to hear all about what you've been up to these past several months."

Cody sat in silence for a moment wondering if he should tell her the whole truth. Then out of nowhere he heard Mrs. Kramer's voice; *utter weariness makes it feel impossible to face a new day.* Cody took a deep breath and decided to tell her everything. The proposition, the surprising birth of baby Madison and being in the delivery room watching Madison take her last breath. Barbra was all ears. She could not believe that so much had transpired in both of their worlds in the past several months. Finally she spoke. "Cody I'm so sorry to hear that. Are you sure you're ok?"

"Yeah, after the third week I finally came to grips with it. And it didn't hurt going to the hospital everyday seeing baby Madison."

"Aw, I bet she's adorable. So are you excited that she's coming home tomorrow?"

"Excited and nervous. But, you know what I'm also excited about?"

"What's that?" asked Barbra.

Cody eased over into her personal space and gently hugged her. He then pressed his lip to he ear and whispered, "having you back in my world."

Cody released from the hug and peered into Barbra's eyes. He could see the tears welling up. In contralto she spoke, "you really mean that?"

"With all my heart," he declared.

"Show me," she countered.

Cody placed his lips atop hers and began to remove her clothes. Soon their bodies became one instrument, making beautiful music all throughout the night.

Chapter 20

After a round of effusive morning lovemaking Cody returned to bed with a bowl of fruit. He fed Barbra grapes, berries and sliced melons. As Barbra basked in the after glow Cody reached over to the nightstand drawer. His hand returned with a small box. "Remember that night at Satl-Mat when I told you I had bought you something?" he asked.

"No way! Is that the same gift?" Cody nodded. "You kept it all this time?"

"I did—hoping one day I would be able to give it to you."

"Give me it!" she said snatching the box. When she opened it her mouth fell wide open. It was a gold necklace with a small heart charm engraved with: 'FOREVER MATCHLESS'...

"Cody it's beautiful."

"Here, let me put it on," Cody offered. After doing such Barbra eased her way back on to Cody's lap to show her appreciation.

***

Later that night they lay with baby Madison resting between them. They both held warm smiles watching her sleep so peacefully. Once the excitement of the day simmered, Barbra lay ensconced in the cuddle of Cody's embrace. "Cody I feel so complete right now. Do you think..." Barbra paused.

"Do I think what?"

"Don't laugh at me ok."

"Depends." Barbra nudged him."

"Do you think I'm... oh just forget it. I feel stupid right now."

"Hey, what have I always told you about that?"

"I know, it's just that I'm at ease when I'm with you, and I don't ever want us to fight again."

"Come here," said Cody pulling her on top of him. "Listen, you're my best friend. I care for you dearly. I haven't told you this, but when I couldn't find you for all those months, I realized that I was in love with you. So what'll you say, wanna be a couple?"

Barbra's expression was blank. She couldn't believe her ears. Since meeting Cody years ago she had pined for this day. "Cody are you being serious?"

"Just say yes and we'll find out." Barbra closed her eyes and gently exhaled. Cody continued, "plus I don't think I can raise baby Madison alone."

When Barbra opened her eyes tears began to escape. Cody wiped at one then gently caressed the side of her cheek. Barbra then went in for a kiss. Once their lips released she spoke, "yes, yes, and yes! I would love to be a couple. And, I would be honored to help you raise baby Madison." Tears of joy were now cascading down Barbra's cheeks. Cody now knew this is where his heart belonged as his eyes too allowed tears to happily flow. They shared in a heart-felt kiss then Barbra spoke, "can we make love now?"

Epilogue

And that they did, over and over, and over again resulting in Barbra having two girls and one boy. They married after their first daughter Codi was born. Now approaching their tenth anniversary they're still very much in love as the day they reunited. Barbra accidentally became a model and is now classified as one of the Top 100 hottest women in the world!

Cody accidentally designed a heat sensor lens for the Z-phone and is now a multi-millionaire and a very sought after man in the tech industry. Dad put up a huge dispute when Cody and Barbra tried to move him into their home. Therefore Cody and the family spend countless hours visiting him at Flowers Manor. With the help of a break through medication he does not blank out as often.

Today Cody and Barbra lay on the beach in Cape St. Vincent watching the sunset. "Wow, this is complete solace, in all of its splendor," Barbra mellowed.
Out of the blue Cody thought back to a toast Madison proposed many years ago. *To blessing you'll receive in the near future.* Cody formed a smile. He then replied, "solace... I totally agree. Right here next to my beautiful wife. What a place to be. I love you Barb. Ten years ago who would have ever thought that you and I were... **Dollars To Doughnuts!**

About The Author

Shakir Mack is an American author and philanthropist from Middletown, Ohio.

Coming Soon...

Nine Days' Wonder

An alluring women's trilogy

by Shakir Mack

Made in USA - Kendallville, IN
91182_9780578243788
02.09.2022 1925